THE GIRL FROM RECOLETA AND OTHER STORIES OF LOVE

THE GIRL FROM RECOLETA AND OTHER STORIES OF LOVE

Jefferson Flanders

Munroe Hill Press
Lexington, Massachusetts

Cover design by Mick Wieland Design

ISBN: 098878405X
ISBN-13: 978-0-9887840-5-5
eBook ISBN: 978-0-9887840-3-1

Munroe Hill Press
Lexington, Massachusetts

For Julie Christina

A thought transfixed me: for the first time in my life I saw the truth as it is set into song by so many poets, proclaimed as the final wisdom by so many thinkers. The truth—that love is the ultimate and the highest goal to which man can aspire. Then I grasped the meaning of the greatest secret that human poetry and human thought and belief have to impart: The salvation of man is through love and in love.

    - Viktor Frankl, *Man's Search for Meaning*

Contents

Introduction

The actor, director, and screenwriter Orson Welles once argued that we are born alone, we die alone, and that only through love can we create the illusion that we are not alone. I think that Welles had it half right—when we love deeply and profoundly, it's not an illusion and we are not alone. It is in those moments of love that we are connected, that we bask in the light in an often dark and indifferent world.

These ten stories are about love in all its forms.

- JF
October 2014

1

The Girl from Recoleta

I fell in love with the elusive and alluring Maria Gabriela Romero Alvarez in exactly the way you might expect an incurable romantic from a small-town in northern Maine would. Head over heels. Blindly, without any reservations. Helplessly. Hopelessly.

At first it was our differences that attracted us. She hailed from Recoleta, the most exclusive neighborhood in Buenos Aires, and she resembled her ancestors from Galicia, dark, petite, graceful, and mysterious—where I was lanky, fair-haired, with Nordic features. I could pass unnoticed on a Copenhagen street.

Her grandparents had emigrated to Argentina from Spain, in 1939, after the Civil War, and she came from a wealthy family—a lavish apartment in Recoleta, a summer home in Punta del Este, trips to Europe. My origins were much humbler. My grandfather Lars Christiansen, a carpenter from Aalborg, set out for America at the start of the 20th century to make his fortune, a goal that eluded him as much as it did my father, a solidly middle class high school shop teacher in Augusta, Maine.

I met Gabriela near the end of my second summer in New York City at a party of graduate school students. My friend Ramon, also training to become an architect, had dragged me along and had introduced me to Gabby, as her friends called her. We began talking, hesitantly at first, but then more easily, as we somehow sensed a deep compatibility and, I found myself hoping, a corresponding attraction.

"And what do you do?" she asked.

"Right now I'm studying bridges," I explained. "Someday I hope to design them."

"Why bridges?"

"I've been fascinated by them since I was a little kid," I explained. "I must have sketched Memorial Bridge in my hometown a hundred times. Eleven arches across the Kennebec."

"Eleven arches? An odd number. Why not twelve?"

"I never thought about it. Perhaps that's all they needed to span the river."

She shook her head. "Twelve is a better number."

I asked about her work.

"I'm also a student. Psychology. I study ways to help people who have been through trauma. To help heal the psychic damage. I work at an institute affiliated with the University where we research new treatments."

"What sorts of trauma?" I asked.

"All sorts," she said, "but it's depressing to talk about. I would rather hear about your bridges."

She asked a lot of questions about what I was studying and seemed genuinely interested when I told her about my focus on Othmar Ammann, the structural engineer who had designed six New York City bridges, including the George Washington Bridge.

"Le Corbusier called it the most beautiful bridge in the world," I told her. "They were going to face the bridge with stone, but the Depression put an end to that idea, because of the cost, and so it's constructed of structural steel."

"We have a bridge made of steel in Buenos Aires," she said. "The *Puente Transbordador del Riachuelo* at La Boca. It's very tall and it had a moving platform, like a gondola. It's no longer used." She smiled. "It's an awkward looking thing, not very beautiful, but it's been preserved for history."

"What about your family?" I asked. "Do you get back to Buenos Aires much?"

"No," she said. "I've been so busy here."

"So do they come and visit here? Your parents, I mean?"

"They're older," she said. "They don't travel outside of the country."

"That must be very hard. To not see them."

"We're not close," she said. "Are you close with your family?"

"I guess so," I said. "We're Scandinavians so you might not think so because we don't express much in the way of emotion. No hugs and kisses or tears or yelling. But I love them and they love me. We just don't say it in words."

"Unlike the excitable Latins?"

"Did I say that?"

She laughed, "No, but you thought it. It's the stereotype, but we're not all like that."

After the party I asked Ramon about her.

"She says she's not close to her family," I explained. "That seemed strange. I thought Latins were all about family."

Ramon shook his head. "Not all," he said.

"So Gabby told me."

"So it's 'Gabby' already. I'm impressed."

"We hit it off," I said. "What about her family?"

"They're not close. In her case there are good reasons. From what I understand, her father was in the Argentine military, quite high up. Her brother followed in his footsteps and is now an officer."

"I don't understand."

"Didn't Gabby tell you what she does?"

"She works at an institute that's focused on therapy for trauma victims."

"Including victims of torture."

"I'm still not following you, Ramon."

"Her father was a colonel in Argentina during the Dirty War, in the late seventies. They did lots of awful things. Disappearances. Torture. Dropping people from airplanes. She would have been five or six years old at the time, and in high school when the truth started to come out."

"Was her father prosecuted?"

"He was not. They never really had justice for that time in Argentina. There's little doubt that he was involved, complicit in what happened. He rose to the rank of general during those years, and how could that have happened without him knowing, if not countenancing those horrors? When she realized his complicity, she confronted him and there were nasty arguments. She took it very hard, moved out. Her grandfather on her mother's side had left Gabriela some money and she used that to come here for college and graduate school."

"How do you know all this?"

"I dated one of Gabby's friends, Fernanda. She's also a *porteña*, and she told me the story." He shrugged. "Gabriela had a sheltered upbringing. Learning about her father shattered that. You don't have to be a psychiatrist to see why she has been drawn to trying to heal trauma victims. It's made her a very unhappy person, I think. All families have secrets, but her family had some of the worst. She's troubled. Doesn't trust easily. Doesn't make many friends, doesn't keep them."

"And men?"

"They don't last long. Or at least that's what Fernanda said."

"So I shouldn't be shopping for an engagement ring?" I asked, making a joke out of it.

Ramon looked at me. "I don't think you're her type."

"How is that?"

"I don't mean to offend. You're too nice, too normal. Too All-American. She likes *los gilipollas*."

I arched my eyebrows.

"Dickheads," Ramon explained with a wry smile. He could see that I was intrigued by her, and I realized too late that he was trying to warn me about her. "And fortunately, or unfortunately in this case, you don't fall into that category."

I fought an uphill battle to win Gabby's heart all that fall. I waged it over midday coffees and romantic dinners, strolls in Morningside Park, visits to museums, long conversations where we talked about everything under the sun. She didn't make it easy, because whenever it seemed I was making progress, she would pull away and make excuses not to see me for a week or two.

But she didn't end it, so I had hope.

She fascinated me, of course, and I think in some ways I intrigued her as well. I was so different from the Argentine men she had encountered.

I didn't give up my pursuit because I could tell that, despite herself, she was attracted to me. There was always something there—the way she tilted her head when we talked, her smile of welcome, her soft goodnight kiss on my lips—that kept me hoping I could win her.

I fell for her hard. I had never known anyone like her. There was nothing predictable or familiar about Gabby. She didn't have her life planned out with a list of accomplishments to be checked off one-by-one when completed—graduate degree, appropriately professional husband, two children, a comfortable home in a leafy suburb and a summer place on Cape Cod. If Gabby had plans for the future, she never expressed them to me.

When I asked about children, she bristled.

"My work is more than enough. I don't need to have a family."

"Think of what you might miss, though."

"Perhaps it seems that way to you. Not to me."

That fall we toured New York's bridges—Ammann's five structures and the other spans connecting Manhattan to the outside world. As I snapped photos and took notes and made sketches, I explained why I was drawn to them, how they represented grace and freedom coupled with the cold beauty of applied mathematics.

The only photograph of us together came from one of those visits. Gabby guarded her privacy fiercely and, at least in my presence, never let anyone take her picture. On a Saturday jaunt to the Brooklyn Bridge we ran into a Port Authority engineer I knew, Hal Bridges (he was a good sport about the inevitable and obvious jokes about his name), who offered to snap a photo with my camera.

To my surprise, Gabby agreed and we posed with my arm draped over her shoulder, the skyline of lower Manhattan behind us. She wore a shy smile as she gazed at the camera, and my face is turned slightly because I was looking at her, and not anywhere else.

As the days grew shorter, and the weather colder, we grew closer. I learned how to read her, to anticipate her dark moods, and to find ways to make her laugh, to lift her out of her funk.

When we finally went to bed, Gabriela insisted on keeping the lights off. It was cold out, a November night in Manhattan, and she stayed under the covers, and so we made love, silently and awkwardly.

I could make no claims to being an experienced lover—I had slept with only a few women—but I could tell that she was holding back, that she was not giving herself to me openly, fully. Afterwards, I touched her face and found her cheeks wet with tears. When I asked her what was wrong, she did not reply, but buried her face in her pillow and refused to answer. I knew better than to press her.

I fell asleep, and when I awoke, she was standing on the far side of the room, her back to me so I couldn't see her face, gazing into a mirror. She had donned her elegant dress and I took in her dark hair cascading over white shoulders and wondered if I could ever love another human being as much as I did her in that moment.

It was not until much later, when I had a point of comparison or two, that I realized how closed-off Gabriela had been. We made love, but always in the dark, and my fumbling attempts at drawing her closer to me, to show her that my desire was mixed with tenderness, were met with resistance. She rejected full intimacy, I decided. Something about it repelled her.

She would not talk about it, of course, and I was afraid of asking her about it. I feared I would lose her if I did.

I wasn't blind to the irony. A graduate student in psychology who couldn't confront her issues with intimacy and sexuality. I wondered if she was in therapy, but that was another question I was hesitant to ask. I stayed silent.

As we saw more of each other, I began to wonder whether it was healthy for her to work at the Institute. It seemed that she was internalizing much of the sadness and pain she encountered there. A few times I found her alone, in tears, and while she refused to explain, it was clear that she was responding to something had happened that day at the Institute.

When I gently raised the topic with her, she turned on me in anger.

"What do you know?" she asked, glaring at me. "What I do at the Institute is the most important thing in the world to me."

"It seems to bring you down, though," I said. "I know you may have personal reasons for wanting to help, but...."

"You have no right," she said. "Have I ever asked you for your views on this?"

I admitted that she hadn't.

"I don't want you meddling in my life," she said. "It's not your place." She stared at me, still angry. "I will see other men. I will not be controlled."

"I can't say that makes me happy."

"That's how it will be," she said. "If you wish to continue to see me."

"Give it some time," I said. "Maybe I can convince you otherwise."

I was young and in love and still believed that I could somehow fix things, or that somehow all would work out, magically. Time heals all wounds, right? That's crap, by the way. The signs were all there, and I just didn't want to see them. Can you blame me?

It was early in the New Year when things fell apart. Although she had said she would see other men, I didn't really believe it. I thought that I had captured her heart, that we had an agreement, unspoken, that we had become "exclusive"—in the awkward phrase that people used then.

So I ignored any signs that she might be restless or dissatisfied until a January night, a Friday, when she had told me she was going away the following weekend with another man, someone she had met recently, a friend of Fernanda's.

It caught me by surprise and I found myself freezing up, not sure what to say or do. Early on I had dreaded that this moment might come, but I had convinced myself that it couldn't happen. But now it had.

"That hurts," I said. "I won't lie. Why are you doing this?"

"You're too calm," she said. "You should hit me. Slap me on my face. Hard. I deserve it."

"No," I said. "I can't do that. You told me that you might see other men. I just didn't think that you ever would."

"So now you know," she said. "You know what I am like, and you should know that if it wasn't this man, it would be another. I don't deserve you, and you don't deserve to be treated this way."

"That doesn't make sense," I said. "You deserve me. I wouldn't be here with you if that wasn't so. You don't care for him, do you?"

"I don't care for him. Not in the way I've cared for you."

"You've a strange way of showing it."

"I warned you. I told you that I would hurt you and you wouldn't listen."

"That's not a reason," I said, doggedly sticking to the rational, always a losing proposition in matters of the heart.

"We're not truly *compatible*," she said. "You're so innocent, with your shining bridges and your romance. It's not the world as it truly is. It's like a beautiful English garden, so orderly and yet so artificial and beyond the hedges there's the pain and disappointment and cruelty—the way people really live."

"They don't have to live like that. We don't."

"I could pretend that your pretty garden is real," she said. "But I know better."

"What's his name?" I asked, surprising myself, realizing how I was sliding into the caricature of the jilted lover.

She shook her head. "Don't embarrass yourself."

"You're making a mistake, Gabby."

"No, the mistake was to believe that this could work. You and me. It can't."

"I don't believe you really mean that."

She turned her face away from me. "You should leave now. Before I begin to hate you. And I really mean it."

And so I did.

After I left her apartment, I wandered around for hours dazed and confused, tears stinging in the frigid air. I tried to understand what had happened to us.

I couldn't shake the feeling that this other man was a pretext to disengage, that she was beginning to care too much and that scared her. But was that my wishful thinking at work?

I didn't get much sleep that night and the next morning I telephoned her and asked if we could meet to talk. "There are some things I want to say to you," I told her. "Before anything more happens."

There was a long silence at her end of the phone and then she finally said yes. I asked her to meet me at eleven o'clock at a coffee house on 115th Street, near Columbia.

I arrived early and, grateful for the warmth of the place, found an isolated table in the back, where we would have some privacy. I ordered a cup of coffee and sat there and thought through all the things I wanted to tell her—how I had never been so captivated by anyone else, how I thought we had a rare connection, and I how I didn't want to lose her. I would ask her to help me understand why she couldn't commit to me the way I was ready to commit to her.

Call me deluded, but I was convinced that I could change her mind and that she would cancel her weekend away, and we wouldn't go on as before but would confront whatever barred us from greater intimacy.

When I glanced up at the clock on the wall, I realized it was later than I thought—fifteen minutes after eleven. I figured that Gabby was running late and I kept inventing excuses for her, but that didn't work when thirty minutes passed, and then forty-five, and she hadn't turned up.

At noon, I knew with certainty that she wasn't coming. I left the coffeehouse and walked through the cold to Riverside Drive, and then to the park, and then to a place where I could see the slate gray Hudson and the sun glinting off the steel of the George Washington Bridge to the north, Ammann's amazing creation.

I stood there shivering and I felt a bleakness, an emptiness, that I hope never to feel again.

A week after she stood me up, Gabriela completely disappeared from New York and from my life. When I called, a metallic recording explained dispassionately that her number had been disconnected.

I went to her apartment building and the superintendent there confirmed that she had left suddenly, and that a new tenant was ready to move into her abandoned apartment.

At the Institute I was politely informed that Maria Romero Alvarez was no longer working there, and had left no forwarding address.

Ramon had been away, visiting his family in Caracas, and when he returned to New York I asked for his help in finding out where Gabriela had gone.

Ramon talked to Gabriela's limited circle of friends, but all he came up with were theories as to her whereabouts.

"Do you think she went back to Buenos Aires?" I asked him.

Ramon looked at me sadly. "You can't be serious," he said. "Buenos Aires? That's the last place on earth that I think you'd find Gabriela. Fernanda thinks she may have gone to Madrid. There's a brilliant psychiatrist there who apparently is working miracles healing those who have faced torture. Dr. Flores. Fernanda heard Gabriela talk about his work, how he was a visionary."

I called Dr. Flores's office in Madrid and finally was connected to someone who spoke English well enough to tell me that no, Miss Romero was not working with the professor, nor with anyone else affiliated with the doctor.

Had she confirmed Gabby's presence, I would have emptied my back account and flown to Spain to confront her, to ask those questions I hadn't asked, to somehow make her deal with me, with us.

I recovered, of course. It took some time, but I got over her. Later, I realized that while she could not give me her heart, she gave me a different gift. She taught me that there were hard questions that had to be asked and answered between lovers—no matter the cost. Far better to expose the emotional fault-lines early on, even when it meant that you had to cut your losses.

Yet there are days, crisp autumn days, when I cross a Manhattan street and see a small dark-haired woman on the sidewalk ahead of me and suddenly feel my heart race as I wonder if it's her, somehow magically returned to New York. It's never her, of course.

I remember that magical fall when we walked hand-in-hand on the Upper West Side and it seemed everyone we passed smiled back at us. Sometimes I'd catch a stranger staring at us—because of the contrast? Fair and dark, tall and short? Or because we were oblivious to everything but each other?

In my heart, I know that Maria Gabriela Romero Alvarez will not be back. I can only hope that as the years have passed, she has won her battle, that she let herself heal, that she opened herself to that deeper connection that we all yearn for. She deserves that, and more, the girl from Recoleta, the love of my life.

2

Secrets

I never thought this would happen, he says.

Never?

I thought you were completely out of my league.

What league is that? she asks, and laughs softly.

You know what I mean. Look at me. I'm not exactly ready for the cover of *GQ*. I figured that if you ever became unattached, that you could have anyone you wanted, and there was no way I was going to be your type.

So you didn't know me at all, but you had figured out that I had a type? And that you weren't it.

Stupid on my part, he says. I shouldn't assume. I mean, Marilyn Monroe married Arthur Miller.

She laughs again. Am I Marilyn in your eyes?

I should just shut up, he says. I'm getting myself in deeper and deeper. What do they say, stop shoveling when you're digging a hole for yourself. I'm going to stop shoveling.

Let me tell you my secret, she says. I knew the first time we met that this would happen. I just didn't know when.

You did? Really?

Yes, really. Do you remember what we talked about? You told me about your reconstruction projects, the ones in the Dominican. You had so much passion about it, but you were practical, as well. You didn't have to talk for too long before I realized how strongly I was attracted. I remember thinking that I wanted you, and wished I could tell you that, right then and there.

If you had, it might have saved us a lot of time and trouble.

Perhaps. But perhaps we needed that time and trouble to get us here, now.

All things being equal, I'd rather have missed that. I wished we had met when we were both much younger and single and everything had been a lot less complicated.

I don't wish that, she says. I had things to learn and experience so that I could arrive here as someone ready for this, for us. I had to discover what matters and what doesn't. I wouldn't have known that then. I wouldn't have fully appreciated you.

Appreciate me? I'm not such a great bargain, you know. Even marked down for the dings and scratches.

You're wrong, she says. You can't see yourself. You're a warm, intelligent, caring man. You're not wrapped up in yourself. You listen to me. That's so much more important than your bank account.

We won't go too far on my bank account. Far enough, I guess.

Here's another of my secrets, she says. Now that we're here, together, I'm not going to do something stupid and lose you. I told myself that if I ever got the chance with you, I wouldn't mess up.

We share that secret, then, he says. I never thought in a million years that we would be together, but if by some miracle it happened, I was going to get it right. I'm going to slow down some, so I have the time for us. I'm not willing to come home to an empty apartment anymore, and if that means letting go, then it means letting go.

If you're in the mood to let go, why don't you let go with me, she says.

I'll always be in the mood when you're involved. And there's nothing secret about that.

3

The Reading

Katya settled on her costume for Alison's Halloween party—Holly Golightly of *Breakfast at Tiffany's*—at the last moment. She knew some of Alison's other friends spent weeks figuring out clever costumes, but Katya wanted something simple. She slipped on a "little black dress," found a string of fake pearls, and bought a cheap plastic tiara from a party store.

When she arrived at Alison's apartment, it was already crowded with party-goers in costumes: an astronaut, a pussycat, a witch, someone dressed as an iPhone (in carefully-painted cardboard), a pirate, two cowboys (no surprise in San Francisco), and a couple in Roman togas.

Alison, dressed as a 1920s flapper, quickly intercepted Katya once she entered the apartment.

"You're finally here!" she began, surveying Katya's costume. "Very cute. You do have a bit of the Audrey Hepburn thing happening."

"I'm here," Katya said. "Happy Halloween, or whatever we're supposed to say."

"Happy Halloween," Alison said. "I have a favor to ask. Could I get you to do a quick reading for a friend? I've told her about your superhuman powers and she's really intrigued."

Katya shook her head, regretting—not for the first time—that Alison knew that Katya had done readings in the past. "I've retired from it," she said. "It's been quite a while since the last one, and I'm out of practice."

"Ridiculous," Alison said. "You have a gift. Don't be selfish, Katya. Share some of your ESP with us."

Katya didn't want to argue with her, or to point out to Alison that her gift—if that's what it was—wasn't ESP.

Alison took her by the hand and led her to the far side of the apartment, where a young woman, dressed as Snow White, waited.

"Meet Mackenzie," Alison announced. "I've told her about you, Katya, and she so wanted to meet you.

"I'm really curious about the process of reading people and what it's like," the woman said, looking at Katya. "Alison says it's amazing what you can see."

Katya shook her head. "I think it's just being a little bit more intuitive," she said.

"Mackenzie would love to have you read her," Alison said.

"I haven't done a reading in ages," Katya said.

"It'd be great if you could try," Mackenzie said.

Katya was annoyed at Alison, but Mackenzie seemed nice enough. She could always tell the woman that she wasn't seeing anything and explain that sometimes it happened that way, that for whatever reason, Katya couldn't make a connection. And the truth was it more likely than not that she would draw a blank.

As a child, Katya had learned to stay silent about her second sight.

When she was five she had a dream where Mrs. Baskin, who lived two houses down the street, floated above the neighborhood like a bird and then disappeared into a cloud. When Mrs. Baskin died a few days later, her mother made her promise not to tell anyone about her dream.

Katya never saw her second sight as a spiritual gift, as did her mother.

"Your aunt Helen had it as well," her mother told Katya just after her tenth birthday. "It's a gift from the universe. Clairvoyance runs in the family as a blessing, although it skipped over me and my sister."

"A blessing?" Katya frowned. She didn't care for the dreams, for the strange emotions and premonitions she sometimes experienced. "I wish it had skipped me, too."

Her mother, who had spent the Summer of Love in Haight Ashbury, gave her a hug and told her not to worry, the universe would make it clear to her in time.

As Katya grew older, she had fewer dreams, and she didn't see the images as clearly. When she read someone, she had to close her eyes and to concentrate, and sometimes the pictures would come through sharply, but other times she saw little, if anything.

In college, she did a few readings for close friends, but she stopped after a while because she found it exhausting and she didn't really like the emotional intimacy it required.

Katya followed Alison and Mackenzie into Alison's small bedroom. They sat cross-legged on the floor.

Katya could tell Mackenzie came from money—her jewelry (a gold necklace, and silver bracelets on both wrists) looked expensive.

Mackenzie seemed anxious; she couldn't keep her hands still and her bracelets kept sliding around and making a clicking sound.

"So you know," Katya began, "I can't read your mind. It's emotions I sense. Someone once told me that I had super-empathy power. If it works, I'll pick up your feelings, and maybe some images."

"If it works?" Mackenzie asked.

"No guarantees," Katya said. "There are times when I feel things, see things, and there are times when I don't. There's no way to know in advance."

"And the future? You can see the future?"

"I can't predict the future," Katya said. "That's something that hasn't happened. Sometimes I can see the paths that someone may about to take. They may not be conscious of their own intentions. I just surface them."

"No tarot cards or Ouija board?"

"Nope. It helps sometimes if I hold an item of yours. Your ring, perhaps?"

Mackenzie shot a look at Alison before she carefully removed her ring and handed it to Katya, who kept it in the palm of her hand. She closed her fingers over it and closed her eyes.

The first image that came into her mind was of a woman crying next to a hospital bed. There was an infant lying still in the bed. Katya opened her eyes and turned to Alison.

"It would be better if we had some privacy," she told her. "It's harder for me to read a person when someone else with a strong aura, like yours, is nearby."

"All right," she said, reluctantly.

Katya waited until Alison had left the room and closed the door behind her.

"What did you see?" Mackenzie asked her, with a note of anxiety.

"It was jumbled," Katya said. "Let's try again." She closed her eyes again and the image of a baby came into her mind, and of a tear-streaked face.

"Did you lose a child?" she asked and heard Mackenzie take her breath in sharply.

"How did you know that? Did Alison tell you about my miscarriage?"

"No, she didn't tell me anything," Katya said. "It's what I'm seeing." She looked at Mackenzie's anxious face. "I think we should stop. You seem upset."

"I'm just fine," she said. "Please go ahead."

"I know how painful memories can be," Katya said. "I really think we should stop."

Mackenzie shook her head. "It's amazing that you saw what you saw. Please continue."

Katya nodded and closed her eyes again. She concentrated and she saw the image of a bearded man in a suit and tie. He seemed unhappy, disturbed by something.

"Is there someone in your life who's unhappy right now?" Katya asked. "A man?"

"What does he look like?"

"He has a beard," Katya said. "Well-dressed. He seems distraught."

"Rollo," Mackenzie said. "You're seeing Rollo? Did Alison set me up by telling you? Is this some sort of twisted joke?"

"We've never talked about you, Mackenzie. It's what I see."

"I don't believe you. Alison must have told you about Rollo. She's the only one who knows about him."

"I don't understand."

"Rollo is supposed to be telling his wife that it's over. That he's chosen me."

"We should stop," Katya said. "I don't want to upset you any more."

"The only thing upsetting me is that you and Alison would screw with me like this. Alison's a royal bitch. I don't know what your story is, but it's sick that you do this." She held her hand out. "My ring," she said.

Katya placed the ring in her hand.

"There's a special place in hell for people like you who take advantage of the vulnerable," she said. "I hope you're proud of yourself."

"You asked for the reading," Katya said. "I gave you an honest reading, and I've never talked to Alison about you or your personal life. I'm sorry that I've caused you any pain."

"You're a very convincing liar," she said. "I guess it goes with the territory. What's the con? Do you get people to pay you for the reading?"

"I've never charged for a reading and I never will." Katya stood up. "I'm going to leave, now."

"No, you stay," Mackenzie told her. "You and Alison can laugh at me behind my back after I'm gone."

She slammed the bedroom door behind her, and Katya blinked back tears. She had never had anyone react so violently to a reading, and she hadn't been prepared for the intensity of Mackenzie's anger.

There was a soft knock on the door and then Alison opened it and came into the room.

"Mackenzie just stormed off," she said. "She cursed at me on the way out. What the hell happened?"

"She didn't like what I saw. She thought you set her up by telling me her secrets in advance. Don't ask what I saw, because I'm not going to share anything with you. This is why I don't like to do readings. I won't do this ever again."

"Hey, I'm sorry," Alison said. "I didn't think she'd lose her cool. I guess she's going through lots of things right now."

"Did you ever wonder what it might be like for me? When I see what I see? The ugly things?"

"Please don't leave," Alison said. "There's someone else I want you to meet."

That someone else proved to be a tall young man, somewhere near Katya's age, wearing a San Francisco Giants jersey and a baseball cap. He had dark curly hair and a broad, open face.

He found Katya on the small deck attached to the apartment, where she had retreated, and approached her with two plastic cups of wine in his hands.

"Are you Katya?" he asked. "Alison sent me to cheer you up."

"What did she tell you? Why does she think I need cheering up?"

He handed her a cup of white wine before responding. "She said something about a mind reading that went wrong."

"Do you think that it's real? The ability to read people's minds."

He shrugged. "Who knows. It could be like the *Matrix*. Our brains have electrical waves. Somehow you're able to pick up other people's brainwaves and translate what you see. That's one theory. I'm sure there are others."

"Are you a scientist?" she asked.

"Hardly. I'm a commercial artist. And I'm not a baseball fan, by the way. I borrowed the Giants jersey from my brother, who is."

She nodded, now quite sure what to make of him. She took a sip of the wine. It was quite good.

"I'm Duncan," he said, extending his hand, giving her no choice but to shake it, awkwardly. "Don't worry. I wouldn't ever want a mind reading. I'd rather bumble my way through life not knowing."

"I doubt you bumble."

"You'd be surprised. In any case, I'd rather believe in free will, just like they taught us in church."

"Do you still go to church?" she asked.

"I do," he said. "I'm old-fashioned about it, I guess. It settles me down. Whenever someone tells my pastor that they don't attend because of all the hypocrites in the pews, he smiles and tells them that there's always room for one more."

"So you consider yourself a hypocrite?" she asked, curious.

"Sure. Aren't we all? I try not to judge others, but it's hard not to. At the same time, I'm good at making excuses for my own failings. That's why I'm big on grace. Not grace that you have to earn, by the way, but grace from God."

"You're big on grace. So you believe in God?"

Duncan nodded. "I do. Truth be told, I didn't have a choice—I felt like He pursued me, made me see the world for what it is." He paused. "I don't talk about this with just anybody, by the way."

"I'm flattered then."

"Just another example of free will. I willed myself into talking about it."

"I agree that we have free will," she said. "I don't think anything is preordained. What I see when I do a reading—some of the future is already there in our minds—pictures, images, of what we would do in a given situation. Just like there are images of the past there. That's what I see. Or at least that's what I think I see."

"You know what image is in my mind?" Duncan asked, smiling. "You having a cup of coffee with me at Caffe Trieste."

"Is that so?"

"A very strong image."

"You don't waste any time, do you?"

"Were we destined to meet here, tonight?" he asked, grinning. "Kismet. Fate. Dumb luck. Who knows? I don't really care. But I'll not waste the chance."

Katya looked at him and wondered whether it was by design that they had met, or simply a random encounter. In the end, what difference did it make? He made her smile.

"All right," she said softly. "Coffee it is."

4

I Don't Care If I Never Get Back

"Who are you?" his father asked, his hooded blue eyes flashing at Colin suspiciously, his craggy features suddenly hard and unyielding.

Colin had always hated his father's reflexive South Boston distrust of strangers. When you weren't part of the clan, you were somehow dangerous, to be carefully measured. It was ironic, Colin thought, that he—Aidan Cassidy's only remaining blood relative—should experience the hostility reserved for outsiders.

"It's Colin," he said, but no sign of recognition dawned in his father's eyes.

"Colin?" He was confused. "You're Colin?"

"I am, Dad. I'm here to see you."

"Who are you?" he asked, now plaintively.

"Your son."

"My son." He was bewildered, confused.

"It's Saturday," Colin said. "I visit on Saturdays."

"Colin," he said. "Yes, you're Colin."

"How did the Sox do, Dad?" Colin asked.

"They won. About time."

"What was the score?"

"Where's Eamon?" he asked Colin, ignoring the question. "When is he coming?"

"He can't come this week," Colin said. Eamon, his father's younger brother, had died eight years before. His father had begun asking for him in the last month or so.

"Maybe Eamon will come next week?"

"Maybe," Colin said.

He had read about Alzheimer's and talked to his father's doctors about the symptoms and the progressive loss of memory, but it was different and unsettling dealing with it in person. The best metaphor he could come up with was that it was like listening to a distant radio station, where some days the signal came through loud-and-clear, and other days all you got was static or the overlapping sound from other stations. He knew that at some point the radio would go silent—his father wouldn't be able to carry on a coherent conversation, or realize where he was, but Colin tried not to dwell on the end game.

Colin had learned to numb himself emotionally whenever he visited his father at the Hidden Oaks Assisted Living Community. At least the place was clean and the staff friendly, even if the oaks did, indeed, remain hidden—from what Colin had seen, there were no trees on the property, let alone oaks.

The last several months had been particularly difficult, because he could see his father slipping away, visit-by-visit, memory-by-memory, and he could see that it wouldn't be long before their shared past would be completely gone. And then, what was he left with? Someone who had once been Aidan Cassidy, but now was an imposter, a stranger occupying his father's body.

When he talked about his feelings with Trish, she had hugged him before speaking.

"You don't have to go over there," she said.

"I still feel that I should."

"You always seem to come back depressed. It's your monthly downer, isn't it?"

"If I don't go, he'll be totally isolated. No visitors. Completely alone."

"Aren't there are the people at the facility? The staff? He sees them every day."

"They're not family."

"You've said that most of the time he doesn't even recognize you. Doesn't know who you are."

"But that's only been recently," he said. "And there will be moments when he's completely lucid."

"Didn't you tell me that you were never close to him when you were growing up? Is this some sort of compensatory thing? Some sort of twisted Irish guilt trip? Because if he didn't give you the love you deserved then...." Trish stopped and flushed. "Forget it. None of my business. Do what feels right to you."

"Maybe it is guilt," Colin said. "What's wrong with that? Guilt's a wake-up call for your conscience, isn't it?"

"How do you plan on visiting him? When he's there physically, but not mentally?"

"I don't know," Colin said. "I just don't know."

On his next visit, to his surprise Colin found his father mentally sharp and completely aware of his surroundings—for the first time in months.

When Colin asked Sophie, one of the caregivers, whether anything out-of-the-ordinary had somehow prompted his father's alertness, she had smiled.

"God works in mysterious ways," she said in her lilting Jamaican accent. "His blessings come and go in his own time. When they come, we should enjoy them."

"It's great to see him like this," Colin said.

"Won't argue with that. He can be crusty, but he can also be a sweetheart."

His father wore his Red Sox cap and lounged in a comfortable chair in front of the flat screen where the Red Sox game was playing.

There was a patch of white stubble on his chin where he hadn't shaved closely enough.

"The Orioles are in town, right?" Colin asked, sitting in the chair next to him.

"That's right. The Orioles. We should be winning, but the damn bullpen's worthless. Can't get an out."

"You've been saying that since I was a kid."

"The bullpen's been lousy since you were a kid. Except for Sparky Lyle. Now there was a reliever."

"I think the ballplayers get better the longer they've been retired," Colin said. "You used to say bringing Lyle on for late relief was like pouring gasoline on a fire."

"Did I say that?"

"I can remember sitting in the right field bleachers, a day game, when you said that. We could see Lyle warming up in the pen."

"He was a damn good player," he said. "Forget what I said then. Never should have traded him to the Yankees." He paused, his face softening. "Liked going to Fenway with you. Hell, I loved it."

"Wished we had done it more often," Colin said.

"Remember the last game of Yaz's career?" he asked, turning from the television screen and giving Colin his full attention. "We were there at the park, Colin. Remember how Yaz jogged around the edge of the outfield, near the stands, smiling, shaking hands. What a great player. Carl Michael Yastrzemski."

"When was that, Dad?" Colin asked, testing.

"It would have been five years before I retired. Must have been October of 1983."

Colin nodded. He remembered the day, remembered how he and his father had sat in the stands and drank beer and ate peanuts and tried to stay warm.

"Maybe the happiest day of my life," he said, tears welling in his eyes. "Along with the day you were born. Going to the ballpark with you that day. Yaz's last game."

"I wish you had said something then," Colin said. "About how happy you were. I never could tell."

"It was obvious," he said dismissively. "Obvious to everyone. You should have known."

On the television screen, the camera had panned to show the crowd singing "Sweet Caroline," the Neal Diamond standard that had become an instant Fenway tradition as a sing-along in the middle of the eighth inning.

"Why don't they sing the real song," his father said, frowning. "What does 'Sweet Caroline' have to do with baseball? Nothing."

"It's just a song, Dad. They're having a good time. No big deal."

"So it's no big deal, is it? Who died and made you king? I think it's a lousy fuckin' song."

Colin remained silent, trying not to overreact to his father's sudden flash of anger, hoping that it would pass.

"If they're going to sing, it should be 'Take Me out to the Ballpark,'" he said. "That's the ticket."

His father had a beautiful Irish tenor, and Colin had loved to hear him sing the old songs, "Danny Boy" and "When Irish Eyes Are Smiling" and "Last Rose of Summer."

His father had a different idea, though. He muted the sound on the television and began to sing.

"Take me out to the ballpark," he sang. "Buy me some peanuts and Cracker Jack, I don't care if I never get back."

Sophie appeared in the doorway, all smiles, nodding her head.

"Sing, Mr. Cassidy," she said. "We so love to hear you sing."

5

Their Indian Summer

Miranda was half-way between Chapel Hill and Asheville, listening to a country station on the radio, when she heard a few introductory guitar chords and then his distinctive, husky baritone voice. She knew it was him, immediately, and as he sang she could feel her eyes misting over and her heart pounding.

The song had a simple arrangement featuring acoustic guitar, drums, and slide guitar, unlike a lot of the overproduced country music she'd been hearing lately. She listened intently to the lyrics, as he sang about a summer love, about falling for a Senator's daughter, a girl from the better side of the tracks. There was a catchy refrain about one last kiss on a Kitty Hawk beach, and she knew without a doubt that he was singing about them.

The announcer made some comment about how he was rooting for the song to move up the charts, because Jack Blackburn was a good ol' North Carolina boy from Wilmington finally getting his break in Nashville.

Miranda pulled her Volvo sedan over to the side of the road and sat there for a few minutes, ignoring the traffic whizzing by, and tried to calm herself. It had been twelve years since they had last seen each other. She told herself that she shouldn't get emotional, and then realized how strange the whole thing was—Jack on the radio, singing about their Indian Summer romance.

She didn't know where to start about Jack and their time together. There was something about him that was different and compelling. Tall, coal black hair, hazel eyes, strong features, and a confidence well beyond his years (he admitted to being twenty-four).

Miranda had asked him once whether he had Indian ancestors, perhaps Cherokee, and he had laughed. "Could be," he said. "My mother's side of the family, maybe. That's where I get my wild streak from. The Kerrs never paid much attention to the rules."

"My family is all about the rules," she had said. "Lots of lawyers. Understanding and interpreting the rules. That's what we do."

"That's why you have money. The people who figure out how to look like they're following the rules while they're bending them, they're the ones making money."

"Money isn't everything."

"Spoken like a rich college girl. Money ain't everything, but it's something. Especially when you don't have it."

"It's not everything, though," she said. "Trust me. It's not enough."

The first time she heard Jack sing was on a Friday night in late May at the Beachside. She had finished the semester, packed up, and driven to the Outer Banks with Georgia that morning, more than ready to start her summer.

The two of them had lined up summer jobs—Georgia at a bicycle shop and Miranda waitressing—but there would be plenty of time to enjoy the beach and to party.

The Beachside was jam-packed that night. Jack played the guitar and sang, backed by a bass guitarist and a drummer. He started with "The Long Black Veil" and "I Walk The Line" and then sang some covers of the Eagles. In his second set, he played his own songs, most with a country-rock sound, and the dance floor filled up. He closed with an acoustic ballad, and it seemed every couple in the place ended up on the floor slow dancing.

He came by their table and introduced himself afterwards. Miranda could tell he was attracted to her, and they began talking and ended up closing the place. He took her back to his apartment three blocks from the beach and they shared a bottle of cheap wine and one thing led to another and they ended up sharing a bed.

Miranda moved in with him a day later and never left. She found herself counting the minutes until she could slip away from her waitressing job and be reunited with him.

Georgia had teased her. "This guy must be something else," she said. "I've never seen you like this."

"He's something."

"Do you take time to talk? Or is it straight to bed?"

"We talk. Jack knows all sorts of things. Not just music. And he reads. Books."

"Books? Not auto repair manuals?"

"He's not a college boy, but he's very intelligent," Miranda said, her face flushing. "I've had enough of college boys in button-down shirts and khaki pants who think they know it all. He's smarter than all of them."

"Who would've thought the next Kris Kristofferson would be hiding in Kitty Hawk, North Carolina? And you've discovered him."

"Maybe I have."

"Just remember that Kris' track record in the romance department hasn't been too great. He's broken some hearts. That's what you get with lead singers."

"It's not like I'm looking to get married," Miranda said. "It's a summer thing. A summer fling. We both know that."

In August, Jack wrote a song for her, which she loved, but he refused to play it for anyone but her.

"It's only for you, for us," he said. "I didn't write it to perform in public. You know that line in that John Donne poem—'Twere profanation of our joys. To tell the laity our love'? Donne got that right."

"You've read John Donne's poetry?" she asked, trying not to sound too surprised.

"Imagine that," he responded with a slight grin. "Miss Calkins, my eleventh grade English teacher, made us read it."

"You can play my song in public," she said. "I don't mind if people know we're together. Why would I?"

Miranda wanted to know all there was to know about him—to memorize his smell, his touch, the feel of his lean body when they were naked together in bed. She ran her fingertips over the scars on the bottom of his chin and his right collarbone, hoping that contact would cause him to tell her their stories, but Jack only smiled.

When she asked directly, he shook his head slowly.

"I've got to keep some of my past private," he said. "I thought girls liked mystery in a guy. Don't they?"

"I'm a woman, not a girl," she said. "And you can't blame me for wanting to know. There's nothing I won't tell you about my past."

"I doubt there's anything shocking," he said. "And if there is, I'd rather not know."

"That's where we're different. I always want to know. Isn't the idea to solve the mystery?"

"But then what?" he asked. "They say when you're performing, you should always leave the audience wanting more. Shouldn't be any different with us."

She thought she understood his reticence. He needed some of who he was cordoned off, protected from the world. She was so willing to open herself up to him that his reserve, his reluctance to reciprocate, hurt.

When he did open up, she couldn't have been happier. While he didn't talk much about his childhood, he did tell her a few stories about his high school days, when he "ran a little wild." He hadn't gotten along with his baseball coach. "I was a pitcher," he explained. "I could throw fairly hard and fast. Once the coach told me not to pitch to this batter, a huge lefty, but I kept the ball really low, down at his ankles. Somehow he managed to golf it out of the park. A long home run. I laughed, because what else can you do? Coach Barnes didn't see it that way. Didn't think I took baseball seriously enough. I didn't last much longer on the team."

Jack had spent two semesters studying music at Cape Fear Community College, but he was tired of sitting in classrooms. He took off and traveled around the country, working odd jobs and singing in bars and honky-tonks whenever they'd let him.

"I played in joints in Louisiana where the bartender kept a baseball bat and a shotgun ready for trouble. The guys off the oil rigs would come in after a month in the Gulf, and if they didn't like your music they'd get nasty about it. I learned that if Merle didn't work, to try Johnny Cash. Trial and error."

"It sounds so exciting," she said. "So carefree."

"I've always loved playing on Friday nights. People are done with the week and they're ready to enjoy themselves. I love to get them up and dancing and singing along. It's a rush, believe me."

"Some of your songs are as good as anything on the radio," she began.

"Some of them?" He laughed. "You're as tough an audience as any of those roustabouts in Morgan City."

"Seriously, have you thought about recording an album?"

"And becoming famous? And playing at the Grand Ole Opry?" He gave her a slight smile. "Sure. Who wouldn't? But I don't ever want my playing to feel like a job. I'm happy enough that people pay to hear my music. For now, that's more than enough."

When Labor Day came, time for her to return to home and then to school, she called her father and told him that she was having such a great time in Kitty Hawk that she had decided to stay a few more days before heading directly to Chapel Hill.

"I had hoped to spend some time with you before the semester began," he said.

"Sorry," she said. "I'll come home for a weekend or two. We can catch up then."

"What about Georgia? Is she staying, too?"

"She is," Miranda said, lying.

A few days later, she telephoned Georgia to confess that she wanted to stay in Kitty Hawk longer.

"I'm not ready to start school," she told Georgia. "Not yet."

"What about registration?"

"I'll drive up for the day. Register, buy the textbooks so I can study here, get everything set up."

"I don't know. Sounds like you're playing with fire."

"Jack's singing at this new club in Wilmington over the weekend. I want to be there for him."

"Why don't you come and stay in Chapel Hill? You can drive back for the weekend."

"No, I want to stay here," she said. "I don't want to leave him. Not yet."

Miranda had never been so mixed up emotionally. She prided herself on being a feminist, on her determination to fashion her own career—as an attorney, following in the family tradition—and she couldn't believe that she was so in over her head with Jack.

She had always had the upper hand in her relationships—she was good looking and smart and men gravitated to her. She didn't feel like she was in control with Jack. Secretly she worried that he didn't care as much for her as she did for him.

If one of her Alpha Chi sisters had ended up in a similar situation, Miranda knew that she would have rolled her eyes and thought that the girl was acting like a fool, an overly romantic fool. But here she was—that girl—and she was dismayed at her weakness, but she didn't want to end it, didn't want to leave him.

She wondered—was this what love was actually like? An overwhelming desire to be with your lover? To give yourself without reserve, to want to be crushed under his weight, both physical and emotional?

It was all very confusing. She felt lost, at sea, with no idea of what she should, or could, do next, other than to live one day at a time, like someone in a twelve-step program.

It was the last week of the month, on a beautiful Indian Summer day, when her father showed up and knocked lightly on the door of Jack's apartment.

"Hello, Miranda," he said. "Can I come in?"

She mutely held open the door so he could enter—aware that he was wearing a light gray suit, dressed for work.

She knew why he had come, and in that moment of recognition she hated him for what he represented. He was there to make the lawyerly case, backed by logic, for why the summer had to end and how it was past time for her to return to school.

"You know why I'm here," he said. "I'd like to talk to you and your friend."

"Jack's gone out for coffee. He should be back any minute."

"I'm here because I'm concerned."

"About my shacking up with a man?"

He smiled. "Sure. I'm your father. Protective instincts and all that. I think you're too young for shacking up, but it's more than that. You're jeopardizing important things in your life."

"I've been studying," she said, defensively. "I'll be able to catch up once I'm back."

"But you're missing classes. How long before that's a problem?"

Before she could respond, Jack appeared at the door. She made the awkward introduction, and Jack put his coffee cup on the kitchen table. He didn't sit down.

"Miranda has a bright future," her father said directly to Jack. "I'm here because I don't want to see her jeopardize it."

"I'm not jeopardizing anything," Miranda said.

"Your father has it right," Jack said, flatly. "You should be back at school, where you belong. This can't work, you being here."

Miranda felt tears welling in her eyes and she gasped slightly. "I belong here," she said.

Jack shook his head. "No, baby, you don't. The summer is over."

"But what about us?"

"The summer is over," he said. "We knew it was going to end, didn't we? Let's not make it any harder than it needs to be." Jack turned to her father. "I've got a few errands to run. I'll let you two have some privacy." He didn't look at Miranda as he left the apartment.

She had packed up her clothes and other belongings in a cold rage, and within minutes they were driving south through Nags Head, toward the bridge. They rode in silence. She had never imagined that Jack would betray her, would side with her father on the side of responsibility and respectability, would let her go without a fight and without a word of love.

An hour into the drive, heading west on US 64, she turned to her father. "How did you find us?" she asked.

He didn't respond, keeping his eyes on the highway.

"I want to know," she said. "Damn you. How did you find us? Was it Georgia? Did she call?"

"It wasn't Georgia," he said, calmly. "In fact, she lied for you quite convincingly when I phoned her yesterday."

"Then who was it?"

"Don't you know?"

"I don't," she said defiantly. "Tell me."

"You won't like it." He paused. "It was Jack. He asked me to come and get you and bring you back to college."

"You're lying. Did you hire a private detective?"

"I'm not lying, sweetheart. Jack called my office. He said that it was time for your summer together to end. He wanted my help, because he couldn't bring himself to end it."

"I don't understand."

"Jack told me that as much as he loved you, he understood full well that he could never hold you."

She shook her head, still not ready to accept what her father was telling her.

He continued, his voice softer. "It made sense. He worried that the longer you stayed, the more you'd see his flaws. The day would come when you went back to us, to school and to your family and the future all of it represents. He wanted it to end before you thought less of him. Those weren't his words, exactly, but that was the gist of it."

"Not his words. Did you help him arrive at that understanding? Because it all sounds like you, not like Jack."

"It's Jack," he said. "In a strange way I can sympathize with him. He wanted you to remember him in the best possible light, while you still carried a torch for him. I can't say I've ever loved like that. Your mother and I were friends first, you know. No grand passion or romantic drama." He paused. "I guess I envy you and Jack for that."

"Jack's a coward," she said, and cursed, hating him and her father for what they had done, their collusion. "If he really loved me, he would fight for me. He'd make something of himself, fix those flaws."

"I wish it worked that way, I really do. But it doesn't."

Miranda never spent another summer in Kitty Hawk and she vowed never to vacation anywhere on the Outer Banks. She couldn't bear the thought of running into Jack—if he was there—and the awkward silence that she imagined would follow.

She heard about him, of course, through friends of friends. He moved to Nashville to write songs and break into country music, and then the story was that he had gone to the West Coast, to Los Angeles.

There was silence for several years. She occasionally wondered where he was and what he was doing, but over time she thought less and less of him. Until there'd be an Indian Summer day, and she'd feel sad and wouldn't want to get out of bed in the morning.

Her therapist had explained that Miranda was reacting to the emotional turmoil that she associated with the last week of September, reliving those feelings. Miranda didn't need to pay someone $100 an hour to tell her what she already knew—her sadness stemmed from Jack and the way it ended and how that choice had shaped her life in ways she didn't particularly like.

If Miranda was honest with herself, hearing Jack's ballad on the radio, out of the blue, had been a shock. Unwelcome. After twelve years, wasn't it a bit ridiculous, she asked herself, to find the memories so troubling?

She rummaged through her handbag until she found her cell phone. She called Georgia, hoping to catch her at home. She was in luck, because her friend answered after the second ring.

"What's up?" Georgia asked.

"A song on the radio," Miranda said. "I was on my way to my father's house when I heard it. It's by Jack."

"Jack Blackburn? That Jack?"

"Yes. His song's about an Indian Summer romance with a Senator's daughter."

"I'm sorry," Georgia said. "I can see why that could be upsetting. On the other hand, it's flattering, isn't it?"

"I guess so," she said. "I'm still a little emotional."

"And you have every right to be. I remember how hard it was for you."

"I know it never would have worked out," Miranda said. "Not in a million years. But there was something there, or I wouldn't be feeling it now."

"What will your father say?"

"He'll shake his head but he'll probably be secretly flattered, even though he was only a state Senator, not the real thing."

"Are you going to say anything to Brian? The wedding's in six months or so, right?"

"I think I have to. The song's good—it may even become a hit—and someone will put two-and-two together and figure out it's me and say something to him. I don't want Brian to find out that way."

"It's been years," Georgia said. "Brian should be okay with it."

"He doesn't know about Jack. We've never talked about past boyfriends or girlfriends."

"What will you tell him, then?"

"That Jack was my boyfriend for a summer when I was in college, and that we had a rough break-up. And he wrote a song about that time in his life and that songwriters exaggerate."

"That's it?"

"That's it," Miranda said, and paused. "I don't trust myself to say anything more. I don't want to make it into a bigger deal than it is."

"Brian's a smart man. He won't push." Georgia paused. "You're sure you're over the whole thing, though? Jack and how it ended, I mean."

"I'm over it," Miranda said. "For whatever that's worth, I'm over the whole thing."

"You don't have to convince me."

"I know, Georgia. You're easy. The hard part is convincing myself. Once I figure out how to do that, then I'll be fine. That's the hard part."

6

The Last Wave

My colleagues know better than to ask about the photo, perched on the window sill where I can see it from my desk. It's a black-and-white photograph of Lucas at play, riding that curling, twisting wave that propels him toward the unseen beach. He's surfing at Rincon, the Queen of the Coast, with its long right point break.

I often study the photograph in its silver frame, a photo taken on a luminous winter day.

Those who know Lucas' story stay silent, giving the image only sideways glances when they come to my office, unwilling to engage my grief. Only strangers comment, struck by his grace and beauty, trapped by the camera in photographic amber.

William Shakespeare lost a son at eleven; Ben Johnson's "sonne" was taken at seven. Shakespeare never directly referred to Hamnet (ah yes, Hamnet, so close to Hamlet, the doomed, tortured son) but Jonson wrote a sonnet that still aches all these centuries later: *Rest in soft peace, and, ask'd, say, 'Here doth lie/ Ben Jonson his best piece of poetry.'*

A child as poetry? My poetry? No, I reject that. Lucas was never my creation in that sense. When we lost him just before his nineteenth birthday, he was his own person.

The Buddha taught that attachment is the source of all suffering, and while I will concede that great pain can come from attachment, I will nevertheless argue that we are less human when we deny our need for connection.

Depression is a silent scourge. By the time Lucas was twelve, we could tell that something was wrong. Nora had argued that it was a moodiness that he would outgrow, and she resisted what she called the "therapeutic maze." But enter it we did, eventually, with psychologists and psychiatrists, and individual therapy and family therapy, and the inevitable psychopharmaceutical solutions that didn't prove to be solutions.

For his part, Lucas wanted none of it. He was happiest in a wetsuit, on the water, waiting for the "off the hook" waves, eager for a ride. He would only quit when it became too dark to surf.

"It's so quiet and peaceful out there," he told me once. "There's only me and the wave. Nothing complicated. I get it right, and I'm in the barrel, the green room. There's no feeling in the world like that."

We ended up home-schooling Lucas. Nora made sure he did the work, typically at night, which left his days free to surf. Overindulgence on our part? I don't think so. I believe it was the one of the few things we got right. We gave Lucas the time to enjoy what he loved to do. Forcing him to sit in a stuffy classroom on a day when he longed to be on his board would have been wrong. I'm sure of that.

It was a mixed blessing for Nora, though. She saw more of Lucas than she ever would have if he had stayed in public school. They grew closer, which meant that his loss was more pronounced, deeper, more painful. But what can you do?

There were a few times when we talked about his depression, the blues, the down moods.

When the conversation strayed into that territory, Lucas would give me the shy smile that he used as a defense, a barrier, a way to evade us, evade the world.

But occasionally he would tell me how he felt.

"It's like swimming with weights around your ankles," he said. "I don't know whether that's the best metaphor. Once in a while I'll sense that it's getting dark, mood-wise. I try to fight it—go for a run, watch a funny movie, anything to get the train off the tracks."

"It hurts?"

"Mostly when I hit bottom," he said. "It must be like drowning, when you can see the sun hitting the top of the sea above you, but you're stuck and can't begin to ascend."

"I hope that's an uncommon feeling," I said.

"Words," he said. "I can't really explain with words. I wish I could let people experience it with me. Not for too long, but long enough to know."

"I'm trying to understand," I said.

"Thanks," he said. "But it's like the story of the blind men trying to describe the elephant. I think that you can't get it, the whole of it, unless you sink to the bottom. And I wouldn't wish that on my worst enemy."

It's no surprise that Lucas sought the sea for his escape.

In the police report, his death is described as a surfing accident, but that's an evasion, a sop to family. Lucas knew the danger of the surf that weekend, how chancy going into the Zone would be, the likelihood of being "worked," of wiping-out and being thrashed around underwater, held under by the force of the wave.

A few people on the beach saw a man on a surfboard paddling out into the Pacific and were surprised anyone would chance the water that day. After a series of strong waves rolled in, the surfer disappeared from view. One of the onlookers called 911, but there wasn't anything the police could do.

Lucas' surfboard washed ashore, but his body never turned up—the storm continued for nearly two days, making an immediate search impossible. I could accept that, but Nora never could. She craved the resolution that seeing him one more time would bring. It was one of the differences that drove us apart.

Nora never forgave herself, or us. Our marriage failed, its binding force—our son—now gone.

I threw myself into my work. I tried therapy. I took a month's vacation and went mountain-climbing in Switzerland, far from the sea.

When I returned, I placed the photo of Lucas on the window sill by my desk.

Could we have done more? Or could we have found a different way to help Lucas?

Who knows? We did the best we could. I've learned that you can chase after the answer, wondering if we had done something different—more intense therapy, better monitoring, more detached parenting—that there would have been a different outcome. But, in the end, there's no answer, no cause-and-effect relationship between doing this or that.

Once, when Nora and I were arguing about something involving his treatment, Lucas must have overheard us. He came into the room and asked us to stop.

"Don't fight," he said. "I know you're trying to help. I know you love me. That's what matters. And I love you both, too."

"If I could trade places I would," I told him. "To make it better."

"It doesn't work that way," he said. "When it's your wave, you have to ride it. No one can take your place."

These days I'm able to stop and watch the surfers at Rincon or Hammonds Reef or Leadbetter Point. It brings back the best memories I have of Lucas, and I've stopped looking for him among the wet-suited young men on their long boards.

I'd like to report that I've made my peace with what happened, but that would be a lie. I've not achieved an other worldly detachment as the Buddhists counsel, nor have I have found solace in any traditional religious understanding of why bad things happen to good people. I'll never completely reconcile myself to losing Lucas.

Whatever comfort I've found comes from knowing that it was the sea that took Lucas from us, that—I like to think—welcomed him home. Didn't all sentient life evolve from pools of organic matter on the ocean floor? Not quite ashes to ashes, dust to dust, but close enough. I tell myself that someday, when the sun begins to sputter out, the depths of that sea will be a haven for the last living creatures on earth.

7

Pillow Talk

Do you feel like talking? she asks.

Sure.

She slips her right hand into his left hand. How was it for you? she asks.

Great. It always is. I'm easy to please, you know that. And for you?

I love being so close. I love being alone with you, and knowing that the door is closed and locked and there's nothing else in the world that matters except you and me.

So that's a 'yes'? It worked for you?

You're such a wise guy, she says and pauses. Do you think we ever really know someone else? How they truly feel?

Is this going to be a philosophical talk? Or a psychological one? You know I'm like most guys, and I just want to doze just about now. Spent. Used up. My shot bolted.

Can you try to stay awake? I do want to talk.

Okay. But don't ask me any tricky questions, because if I'm half-asleep my answers may not make any sense.

Nothing tricky, she says. Do you think you know how I feel?

What's the right answer?

Stop. I'm being serious, and you just want to joke.

Do I know how you feel? he asks, and pauses. Sometimes I think I do, and the other times it's a total mystery to me where you're coming from. But isn't that a Venus–Mars thing? I can never remember which planet men are supposed to be from.

You're from Mars, she says. We're from Venus. I don't think it's just a male-female thing. It's hard enough for a woman to understand another woman.

Are there feelings of yours that I should know about? he asks.

She sighs. I guess so. Do you think that other couples have had this conversation? In the past, I mean. About whether they could know the other person's heart?

I'd think so, he says. Law of large numbers. Had to come up in the pillow talk of billions of humans since the Neanderthals. Of course this specific pillow talk is going to be unique. I'm going to say the name 'Mookie Wilson' and I'm pretty sure that hasn't been part of a serious talk about intimacy ever before.

Who's Mookie Wilson?

He's the New York Mets player who hit the grounder that Bill Buckner bobbled back in the '86 World Series. Buckner fields the ball and steps on first and the game and the Series is over, and the Red Sox win. He doesn't, they lose Game Six, and then the next game, so they blow the World Series. Red Sox fans blame Buckner, but that's not fair.

You're a funny man, she says. But sometimes that gets in the way, you know?

I know. I deflect with humor. But that's just how I am. You must know how I feel about you, that I love you. Isn't that enough?

There are times when I'm scared or lonely or blue. I want you to know that, to know how I feel. The other day, when we went on that walk, and the sun was shining the way it does this time of year and we passed that bakery and I could smell the bread, and you were holding my hand tightly, I wanted it all to last, to never end. I wanted us to live forever. It seems so unfair that we have to die. That we can't walk past that bakery on a fall day forever and ever. Does that make sense?

It makes sense. I don't know why it all has to come to an end, why the limit to our time. If there's a God, I'd like to ask him about that. But I'll be happy to keep walking past that bakery with you for as long as we can. Fair enough?

Fair enough. No more questions. I'll let you sleep, now.

I'm here for you, he says. Come hell or high water, I'm here for you. That's something never to forget.

8

Princess

There is a legend in our family that the first Kincaid in the New World, Jonathan, married an Indian princess. In fact, Jonathan Kincaid was a bit of a sketchy character—he arrived in Massachusetts Bay Colony some fifteen years after the Pilgrims and only one step ahead of the Lincolnshire sheriff who was looking to arrest him for his considerable unpaid debts—so it's hard to know what to believe.

My great aunt Estella laughed when, at the age of twelve, I asked her about our princess.

"Princess? Jane Kincaid was no princess. She was a Penobscot, I'll grant you, but she was a squaw, plain and simple. The only reason we know anything about her is that she turned up in the court records for quarreling. She had an argument with one of the neighbors and tried to bite her ear off and got hauled before a judge."

"Then why are there stories that she was a princess?" I asked, puzzled.

"We live in a fallen world, Teilhard King Kincaid," she said, relishing the chance to say my full name out loud. Around the time of my birth, my father had been captivated by the writings of Pierre Teilhard de Chardin, this French Jesuit philosopher, hence the first name. King is my mother's maiden name, and what people call me.

"What does that have to do with Jane Kincaid?"

"In a fallen world, people care about the wrong things. I've no idea whether Jane Kincaid was a good wife to Jonathan or a shrew. She certainly had a temper. But back then, for an Englishman to marry a woman with red skin, there had to be an explanation. The easiest was to say that she was royalty."

"And that made a difference?"

"They used to claim during Jim Crow days that if you put a turban on a Negro, he would be warmly welcomed at the finest country club in Richmond, Virginia. As long as they believed he was a foreign dignitary, maybe an Arabian prince, they could overlook the dark skin."

"I don't get it," I said, shaking my head.

Estella nodded. "Shakespeare claimed a rose by any other name smelled as sweet, but he was obviously wrong. Even today some of your Kincaid relatives cling to the idea that Jonathan married into the native royalty. For all we know, he bought her with some beads." She peered at me. "Women were in short supply, you know. They died early, too. And Jonathan was hardly a paragon of virtue. He turned up in those court records a time or two, usually for sharp business practices."

"I don't think you should pay attention to what other people say about who you want to marry," I said. "It's not their life."

"So will you marry a pretty girl who looks like Pocahontas?" she asked me, teasing. "Or will you stick to the girl next door? Blonde hair and blue eyes?"

"I don't know," I confessed. "But I'll make up my own mind."

"You have to give Jonathan some credit," she said. "He had courage. He could have just shacked up with Jane, but he made her an honest woman." She paused, lost in thought for a moment. "That's more than we can say for some of our American so-called heroes. Thomas Jefferson fooling around with his slave, Sally Hemings. Sam Houston and his Cherokee maidens. General Douglas MacArthur with his Filipina actress girlfriend. They wanted to have their cake and eat it, too. God forbid they tell the truth about the woman they loved."

I liked talking with Estella. She treated me like an adult, and I could always count on her to speak her mind, a mind which stayed sharp well into her eighties.

She spent most of the year living on Martha's Vineyard with another woman, Dolores Campion, who had been a famous professional tennis player in the 1920s. Estella had been widowed when her husband died on the first day of the Normandy invasion in 1944—she had moved in with Dolores a year later.

The New York papers said nothing about Estella when Dolores died, even though they had spent the past thirty years together, for better and for worse. Estella made sure that in her own obituary that the *Vineyard Gazette* described her as "the faithful life companion of Dolores Campion." Estella was another Kincaid who cared little for convention.

When in the tenth grade I saw the movie *Ivanhoe*, I couldn't understand why Ivanhoe, as played by Robert Taylor, would ever have consciously chosen Rowena, a pale Joan Fontaine, over the dark, mysterious, and alluring Rebecca, Elizabeth Taylor.

Rowena was polite and passive and had zero sex appeal, and Rebecca, the healer and mystic, the opposite. It was brilliant casting, because if you actually read Sir Walter Scott's novel (I did), it's clear that at some level he believed that Rebecca was the better choice, and I don't know that there's an actress in the world who could have outshone Liz Taylor in 1952, when they made the film.

As it turned out, I didn't end up with Rowena, or anyone like her.

Takara Ishikawa fascinated me from the start. The daughter of Japanese immigrants who grew up in Southern California, Takara spoke fluent Japanese, but also attended UCLA and loved the Beach Boys. She was an appealing mixture of the familiar and the mysterious. And I suspect I was the same for her (although I doubt I seemed that mysterious).

I never understood the stereotype about Asians and inscrutability. As we spent time together, I discovered that Takara's moods and emotions quickly flickered across her face. Today, after years together, I can read the subtle but expressive changes that signal her unhappiness or joy or tenderness.

Strangers always remark on Takara's physical beauty—and I admit it was what first drew me to her—but at some point that becomes a given, and what matters are the other aspects of your beloved. I know that beauty being only skin deep is a cliché, but I'm fortunate that Takara's loveliness has proven to be of the far deeper kind.

So where does this attraction to the Other come from?

My college buddy, Sam Espinosa, who went on to get a master's in marine biology, had his own theory. He introduced me to the concept of genetic interchange. Sam spent a year studying male dolphins in Sarasota Bay and learned that they're very territorial and guard their females fiercely. Yet, despite that, when the scientists took DNA samples they found that ten percent of the dolphin newborns were fathered by dolphins from outside of Sarasota Bay.

"Interlopers," Sam explained. "Somehow, even when she's closely guarded, the female finds a way to mate with an outsider. It's nature's way of upgrading the gene pool. You find it in all mammals. Genetic interchange."

"All mammals?" I asked.

Sam smirked. "Including humans. That fact hits most guys where they live. If you go into any hospital maternity ward you'll find that for about eight percent of the babies the DNA doesn't match the father's name on the birth certificate."

I must have looked skeptical, because Sam pressed on. "I know,

I know, it's a very reductive theory. And it's disturbing from a male perspective in some ways. What guy likes the idea that his newborn may not share his DNA? It's the punchline from the old joke where the rabbi explains why Jewish identify is matrilineal: 'At least we know who the mother is.'"

He punched me lightly on the arm. "Your ancestors had good reasons for taking a walk on the wild side. Both of them. And you wouldn't be here if they hadn't had that urge to merge, would you?"

Aunt Estella didn't care much for her younger brother, Alexander Kincaid, my grandfather. She regarded him as a bit of a pompous stuffed-shirt, but she told me once, she did admire him for marrying a foreigner and for producing three sons.

"He's done his bit for the Kincaid family tree," she said. "Bringing in some new blood into the line with Karin, and having boys."

"And why should that matter?" I asked. "Does the world really need more Kincaids? Or the Kincaid line?" I hoped to provoke her, to see what she would say.

"Careful what you wish for, King," she said. "Your existence is a direct result of my brother's virility. The Kincaid line stretches back to Lincolnshire because the Kincaid men observed the Biblical injunction to be fruitful and multiply. We helped build this country, fought for it, and kept adding branches to the family tree. On the whole, a good thing."

"That's a pretty good argument," I said, smiling.

"Don't smile at me," she said with a mock scowl. "You'll need to do your part when the time comes. Not that any red-blooded Kincaid man ever objected to that duty."

Although Estella did not live to see it, I think she would have appreciated my choice of Takara, and how, in a way, it represents an updating of the Jonathan Kincaid legend. It's likely that our two boys resemble the four sons of Jonathan and Jane Kincaid—Jonathan, Asa, Elijah, and Jeremiah—a blend of European and Asian features. If Jimmy or Ken were transported back in time to late 17th century New England, and met their Kincaid ancestors, I believe that all would be amazed by the family resemblance.

I can also imagine that Estella, if ever asked to weigh in, would disagree. She'd argue that there would be nothing surprising about such a cross-generational reunion, because when it comes to branches on family trees, there's nothing new under the sun. I'd tease her about mixing metaphors, but in the end I'd have to concede that she was right.

9

The Damnedest Things

Ethan had reached Penn Station earlier than usual, so he bought
himself a cup of coffee at Zaro's and found a seat in the Amtrak
waiting area on the Seventh Avenue side of the building. He didn't
want to waste the forty minutes or so before his train, so he decided
he would begin grading the midterm exams his students had
completed that afternoon.

He took a few tentative sips of his coffee and arranged the blue
books in a small pile on the seat next to him. The waiting room
wasn't crowded; the usual early evening gathering—a few students
with backpacks and their ubiquitous iPods and headphones, business
travelers in tailored suits hunched over laptops, a few older couples
chatting quietly (probably retirees who preferred the more leisurely
mode of travel by train.)

He turned to the task of grading, something he had never
enjoyed. He had a smaller class for the fall semester—twenty-six
students according to his official green-colored computer printout
in his leather travel bag—and he figured he could finish some of
their midterms before the boarding call for his train, the Vermonter,
at 6:45, and then polish off the rest during the train ride. Ethan
appreciated the historic train names—the Keystone, the
Pennsylvanian, the Adirondack (which he recalled was the train to
Montreal from New York), and the train he would take, the
Vermonter, which originated in St. Albans and terminated in
Washington, D.C.

The grading went slowly. He had asked his students to write a brief essay on an assigned short story, Judith Rossner's "116th Street Jenny." The first few essays he read were disappointing—the students had concentrated on the surface themes, but had barely touched on the dynamics of the struggle between parents and child at the heart of the story. He labored over the comments at the end of the first few blue books, trying to balance his criticism with some praise, knowing how overly sensitive many of his students could be, most raised in a suburban culture of advantage and entitlement.

"Ethan?"

He looked up when he heard his name, caught off-guard. He found an attractive blonde woman, perhaps in her mid-thirties, standing in front of him, smiling at him, a warm smile of recognition. She seemed familiar—he felt that he should know her—and yet he couldn't immediately place her.

He smiled back, stalling for time, noting in a glance that she was well-dressed, tastefully, expensively. Then, with a start, he realized who it was—Rachel Korr, his first serious girlfriend, his first lover. He had not seen since the afternoon of July 4, 1986 when they had bumped into each other at the corner of Mill Road and Main Street in Durham, their hometown, a few hours before the town fireworks.

"Rachel," he said, and then, in apology for the delay in greeting her. "It's been a long time."

"More than twenty years," she said. "But I would have known you anywhere. I saw you from about fifty feet away and realized immediately that it was you, Ethan."

The sound of her slightly husky voice brought bits of the past back—the hours they had spent together as kids, her trick of finishing his sentences, the impulsive way she would, out of the blue, kiss him. He rose to his feet, remembering his manners, finding that he towered over her—in his memory she was taller. He breathed in the light rose fragrance of her perfume, struck by the elemental appeal she still held for him.

He glanced over at the large diamond ring on her left hand—no surprise that she was married. Rachel had always magnetically attracted men; he remembered how jealous he had been of her, and how he had hated it when she laughed at his poorly concealed jealousy. He had sworn then that he would learn to mask his emotions.

"Don't get up," she said. "I'll sit."

She took the empty seat next to his right, tucking her tailored skirt under her, and Ethan returned to his own spot, trying not to stare at her still-shapely legs, wary of the memories they might stir.

"You haven't changed," he said. "You look—amazingly well, I think, is the technical term." They both laughed; he was embarrassed at how trite it sounded.

"Well-preserved?" she said. "Is that what you mean?"

It was true, she had aged well. Rachel had kept her figure and he could see only slight wrinkles around the eyes and no telltale middle-aged puffiness in her face. He would have guessed that she was in her mid-thirties if he didn't know better—they were both forty-five (although she was actually two months and three days older than him; he had teased her about being an "older woman," when they were dating).

She looked better than he did, he thought: he'd added twenty pounds in those two decades, most of it in his midsection. When he shaved in the morning, he found the physical signs of mid-life beginning to surface in the mirror in front of him—gray hair at his temples, deepened worry lines, perhaps a hint of resignation in his face. And there was his knee, always a reminder of the limitations of orthopedic surgery before the invention of arthroscopy. His knee still stiffened up whenever he spent too much time on his feet. At least, he thought ruefully, he wasn't balding.

"Not quite," he said. "I meant the years have been particularly kind to you. That's a more literary way to say it."

"Thank you for the compliment. And what are you doing here tonight?"

"Waiting for the train to Philly. The Vermonter."

"So am I," she said. "Do you live there? In Philadelphia?"

"I do. In Chestnut Hill, actually."

"So what brings you to New York?"

"I'm teaching this semester at NYU." He motioned to the blue books stacked beside him to his left.

"Teaching?"

"American literature. The short story. I come to New York once a week."

"Are you really an English professor?"

"Couldn't you tell from my tweed jacket? It's standard issue." He smiled at her, trying not to sound defensive at the surprise he heard in her voice. "I guess it would be a bit of a shock. Who would have thought that Ethan Snowe, townie jock, could be teaching literature some day?"

"It's not that, Ethan. I always thought you would be successful in whatever you decided to do for a living. I just didn't think you would want to teach, especially with the way you felt about the snobs at the University. In the old days."

He nodded: they both knew it wasn't his feelings about University snobs, whoever they were, that she was referring to, but how he had felt about her parents, both academics, bookish intellectuals. They had always held Ethan in low regard. When Ethan had tried desperately to follow the Korr's dinner table conversation about books, and politics, and the arts and had failed to keep up, they had treated him with cool disdain. Rachel's father, Nathaniel Korr, a well-known political science professor, had made it clear that Ethan did not measure up as a boyfriend, let alone as a potential son-in-law. It went without saying that Rachel was destined to marry a doctor or a lawyer or a professor, an educated man, Jewish, someone who would be comfortable lighting candles at the Korr's Passover seder. Not a townie jock.

"Where are you headed?" he asked.

"Same as you, Philadelphia. I'm visiting my sister. Wynnewood, actually."

"How is Sara?"

"Sasha," she said, correcting him with a smile. "Sasha is well. She's married. No longer little Sasha. They have twin girls, now seven, who expect their Aunt Rachel to come and spoil them every so often."

Ethan tried to summon up Sasha's face; all he could picture was a skinny little girl, perhaps nine years old. Rachel had claimed that Sasha was jealous; that her younger sister had a crush on Rachel's unlikely conquest, the football captain and hometown hero (a hero at least in the hardware store and barber shop and American Legion bar).

"My memory is shaky when it comes to names," he said. "It takes me all semester to learn my students' names."

"Sasha will be so excited when she hears that I bumped into you," Rachel said. "She always blamed me for losing you, her all-time favorite of any of my boyfriends."

"That's not the way I remember it," he said. "I thought you wanted to lose me."

"A mistake," she said. "Didn't I admit that? Didn't I suggest that we get back together after that first year of college when we were apart?"

"I wasn't particularly receptive to the idea."

"You were bitter."

He wasn't proud of his part in that awkward conversation, and it suddenly didn't seem like twenty years had passed. He hoped he wasn't blushing—his usual reaction to being embarrassed. Rachel had come back to Durham for the summer, and on her first night home they had argued in the Korr's living room; he recalled Rachel's face pale and drawn against the dark Scandinavian furniture as he had made his case why it was over between them. He had never liked the room, it was dark and the walls were lined with built-in bookcases, overflowing with books, and he had always felt intimidated there. He had said some very nasty things—wanting to hurt her, driven by a mixture of resentment and longing—and she had finally asked him to leave.

He had still wanted her, desired her, missed her desperately, but his pride wouldn't let him admit his need. At the time he was in physical therapy twice a week, limping badly, angry that the one thing he was very, very good at had been taken away from him (taken away for good, it turned out, and it was years before he recognized that it was, indeed, for his good.) So they didn't see each other again that summer and he told himself that he had made the hard, but correct, choice.

He attempted a smile. "There was a lot going on. I was at a low point and I didn't think I could hold onto you. And maybe I was too proud. A common male failing."

"So I've heard."

"I'm sorry if I said some harsh things. I sort of remember that I did. I was trying to push you away."

"You accomplished that. 'Heartless bitch,' I think was the phrase you used."

"Forgive me, Rachel."

"You're forgiven. It was a long time ago."

They fell silent for a moment.

"So you enjoy teaching?" she asked, steering the conversation to a safer topic.

"I do. I love it when I can see that a story is opening the eyes of a student, that they can see the world in a different way."

"You always loved stories, didn't you?"

"My mother was an O'Brien, remember? I may have been descended from dour Yankees on the Snowe side, but it was all poetry and stories and blarney on my mother's." He glanced over at her. "And what about lawyering? How has that been?"

"I've practiced on and off," she said. "Jake is the one who loves the law. My husband."

"No lawyers in my family," Ethan said. "My wife designs and makes jewelry."

"That must be rewarding."

"Rewarding? Artistically, perhaps. Not financially."

"Children?"

"I have a son, fifteen. And you?"

She shook her head. "I didn't marry until I was thirty-five." She shrugged. "I think Jake was relieved, frankly. About not having children. He prizes his independence."

"And were you? Relieved?" He wondered for a moment if it was too personal a question; he tried to remember what his Rachel, the Rachel of 1981, had thought about having children.

"I have regrets, sure. But that's not the way it worked out. Does your son play football?"

"Alexandro? No, actually he plays the guitar. He isn't making his dad's mistakes."

"The guitar? I don't remember you as being particularly musical, Ethan."

"Marisa is, though, and Alexandro takes after her in that. He has his own band. 'Emo' I think they call it."

"This is surreal, you know," she said. "That we are sitting here having this conversation. Ethan Snowe, in person, sitting next to me after all these years. What is even stranger is that it seems just like yesterday in some ways."

They were interrupted by an announcement that the Vermonter was ready to board—at Gate 12, the stern female voice explained—and there was the customary flurry of activity as passengers flocked to the open gate. Ethan carefully packed his blue books in his leather briefcase, and the two of them followed the crowd to the gate, waiting together silently to take the escalator down to the platform where the train waited. It wasn't even a question, Ethan thought, but that they would travel together—clearly they both had more to say.

When they reached the platform and boarded the train, Rachel suggested that they sit across from each other. They claimed facing seats next to the front of one of the cars. Ethan put her traveling case in the overhead rack and placed his leather bag on the seat next to her. The train was relatively un-crowded, but he didn't want to be disturbed. They sat facing each other and waited for the departure of the train.

"Do you stay in touch with anyone from Durham?" she asked. "From high school?"

"No, can't say that I do. No reunions. My parents are both gone. Whit lives in Southern California, of all places. Said he never wanted to suffer through another winter. He's a cop, following in Dad's footsteps."

"I'm sorry about your parents. I didn't hear about either of them at the time. Just later. I hope it wasn't too hard."

"Thanks," he said. "It's been a while now. It's something you eventually accept. And your folks?"

"Still alive. Retired. Living in Miami. I know, it's a cliché, isn't it, but they like the sun."

"Do you see them much?"

"Not often. Jake doesn't care much for them."

He couldn't keep from smiling. "Your husband rises in my estimation."

"Jake doesn't particularly respect academics," she said. "They're not doers, and their compensation reflects that fact."

"He's right on both counts." He paused. "I certainly haven't made a great deal of money teaching. We scrape by."

"Money isn't everything. Are you happy?"

"Happy? We have our ups and downs, like everybody does. It's different when there's a child involved. Your life revolves around that."

He didn't want to say any more. How could he describe his life, his marriage, in a way that Rachel would understand? He loved Marisa and yet his marriage had evolved into one of established roles and routines, trading passion for comfort and a quiet acceptance of whatever was missing or flawed in the relationship. Or was that too harsh? Sometimes he believed it just the natural cooling off that any couple experienced with time and familiarity—but he missed the sparks of their early days more than Marisa did, he knew.

The train slowed, brakes squealing as it made a brief stop—the intercom announcing their arrival in "Nork"— and they fell silent as a few passengers boarded, the door behind them clacking open loudly. Rachel waited until they were underway again before she spoke.

"This is a strange conversation, you know. But under the circumstances, it would have to be, wouldn't it? I'm feeling a bit disoriented."

"I am, too," he said.

"So tell me. Have you thought about me at all over the years?"

"Sure. Whenever I hear 'Sweet Baby James' on the radio."

"And how often is that? Do you listen to an Oldies station?"

"Often enough, I guess. I always wonder how you are when I hear that song. *Mémoire involontaire.* Involuntary memory."

"I'm impressed," she said. "With your French accent."

"Don't be. I don't speak French very well. I limped through enough classes to meet my language requirement. That's it."

She brushed a stray lock of her hair back and gazed intently at him, almost as if she was trying to memorize his features, Ethan thought. Or perhaps she was looking for something else in his face—a reminder of the boy she had once loved?

"I am amazed at how easy it is to talk to you," she said. "I should stop saying that, but I had forgotten how easy it was."

"I've suffered with that my entire life. People ask me for directions on the street. Strangers want to tell me things. Maybe I should have been a priest."

"I don't see you as a priest," she said lightly. "Too much sex appeal."

"Thanks. You're going to make me blush. It's that repression thing."

"I loved making you blush when we were kids. It was irresistible. You tried so hard to appear tough and rugged and I knew better. I could see the soft side." She paused. "What about your memories? Do you remember the last time we saw each other?"

"I do. July Fourth. What was it, two years after I finally graduated college? I think you had started law school."

"You were very distant. Not showing your soft side, then. I've always wondered why you were so cold to me."

He remembered, but from his perspective she had it backwards. Rachel had been the distant one, unattainable, confident, destined for success, as they faced each other on the Mill Road sidewalk, just by Main Street. They had run into each other by accident and it had been awkward. He didn't know what to say. He figured that his father and Whit had been right, that she wasn't right for him. So he had been overly polite, reserved, and—if memory served—he had cut the conversation short. That night he had finished two six packs with his buddy Stewie, and in the morning he didn't remember much of the fireworks, or of his brush with Rachel and his past.

"I'm a Yankee, remember? Frozen emotionally. It's taken me twenty years to thaw out."

"Are you thawed now?

"Not completely, according to my wife. Certainly not by Costa Rican standards."

"You know, Ethan, if there had been a glimmer of any feeling on your part that day, I would have come after you."

He shook his head. "I don't think that would have worked. I wouldn't have been willing to take the chance and have us fail. Not again. I had already had enough disappointment, thank you much."

"There was something there for us, though."

"Always was."

"I remember how we were crazy for each. Couldn't keep our hands off each other? Do you remember? That night in Portsmouth?"

"I remember."

He looked away, embarrassed by his memories, the sudden image of Rachel's naked body, her skin pale in the darkened room, her arms pulling him close to her, responding to his lovemaking. It had been her idea, their initiation into the mysteries of physical love that January of their senior year in high school. Rachel had insisted on the hotel room in Portsmouth; she wasn't going to lose her virginity accidentally in the back seat of a car or rolling around on a living-room floor. Ethan remembered the awkward negotiations with the suspicious desk clerk, and how he had fumbled with the lock when they finally reached the room. But there was also the wonderment at discovering how gracefully matched they were—after all their shared anxiety and nervousness—when they were finally alone behind that locked door.

"This is a bit awkward," she said. "I shouldn't have brought it up. We probably shouldn't be talking about this."

"No, we shouldn't. But we are."

"There was a second chance we missed," she said. "I wrote you a letter. After I finished law school. Asking whether you had any feelings left for me, whether we had any chance at all of making it together. I never mailed it."

"That would have been just after I started graduate school," he said. "Still trying to find my way."

"What would you have done? If I had sent the letter."

"I don't know. Rachel, remember my Dad's saying—the past is a different country? There's no way to know."

"What sort of a life would we have had? If I sent the letter, and you had taken that chance."

"That's a massive 'if,' you know. I don't think either of us were really ready to settle down. I was still trying to figure out what I was going to do with my life. So maybe it wouldn't have lasted. Maybe we would have driven each other crazy."

Would she have stayed with him? When he moved to Charlottesville for graduate school, he had still been unsure about what he wanted to do with his life. It was too easy to believe, years later, that their head-over-heels love would have lasted, to think that they would have stuck it out together through the reality of cramped graduate student housing, and too little money, and the accumulated resentments of any new marriage, exacerbated because they would have been so young.

The conductor passed through their car, announcing that the next stop would be Trenton. They had been so deeply engrossed in conversation that Ethan hadn't noticed the train stopping at MetroPark.

"What are you thinking?"

"It's easy to forget what stood in the way, then. The fact that I'm not Jewish. It mattered to you then, I think, quite a bit. Hell, it may still matter. Is your husband Jewish?"

She nodded. "Jake Goldin. I still go by Rachel Korr, professionally. I had boyfriends who weren't Jewish. After law school."

"But you didn't marry any of them."

"I didn't."

"What does that say?"

She laughed. "I'll concede the point. But that was a long time ago. I've changed my thinking about it. I think my parents had it all wrong."

"It's strange that we ran into each other tonight," he said. "The short story I had my students write about for their midterm has always made me think of you and your relationship with your parents. '116th Street Jenny.' Whenever I assign it, I wonder about you and your life."

"Why is that? What is the story about?"

"A young girl, a college student, in New York City whose parents are academics at Columbia and are very controlling. Part of the story is about how the girl, whose name is Caroline Weiss, decides to stand up to them, to assert her independence. That's part of the story, at least."

"Ouch," she said. "Is that meant to hit home?"

"I didn't pick the story knowing I'd see you tonight. I'm not a psychic. But now that you mention it, I guess there's a certain poetic convergence to it."

"Perhaps there is. Why is she called Caroline if the story has Jenny in the title?"

"It's convoluted. There's an artist in the story; she paints a portrait of Caroline and calls the painting '116th Street Jenny.' She gives the painting to Caroline and it takes on a symbolic value for everyone in the story. The artist, her parents, they all want to own or control the painting, and Caroline won't give that up to them."

"I'll have to read it."

"You may not like it. My wife didn't."

"What's your wife like? I've wondered over the years who exactly you might end up with. The type of woman you would marry."

"Marisa isn't a type. She's one of a kind."

"I'd like to meet her. We could compare notes."

Ethan shook his head, smiling slightly. "I don't think so. She's very Latin about that sort of thing."

"She knows about us?"

"Of course. Isn't that part of the courting ritual? The recitation of past loves? The road not taken?"

Rachel shrugged, arching her eyebrows, and Ethan was transported to an August day in the summer before they both went off to college, a day when she had told them that it would be better if they both dated other people that fall. Better for what, he had asked? She never really answered him and she had shrugged in the same expressive way when he had asked if there was any hope that they might stay together.

"Not with Jake," she said. "He never expressed much interest when we were dating in hearing about my ex-boyfriends. Not worried about the competition, I guess. He's a very secure man."

"Good for him. I wish I could say that about myself. That I was very secure."

"You are secure," she said, surprising them both with her fierceness. "You're secure in the right ways. I can tell. But you always were, even when you didn't know it. Jake takes a lot for granted in life. Perhaps too much. I wish he had been more curious about my past."

"And yet…"

"And yet I'm with him. He does love me, Ethan, as unreservedly as he can, raised as he was. Why does money make people so repressed? I call him my Goldin boy, and even Jake smiles at that. He knows that it's true, he's the Golden Boy."

"I recall you being a bit of a Golden Girl yourself."

"Perhaps. Life has a way of knocking those golden edges off. To mix my metaphors. I've lived through my hard times. Scars and tears. Enough to make me wary."

"I would never guess that."

"It shows a little, doesn't it? Don't I seem different today than I did then? Not just older? Changed? Mellower?"

"In some ways. In others you haven't changed at all—and I mean that as a compliment."

"Thank you."

"I don't remember, Rachel, did we ever decide whether it counts as a compliment if it's true? Didn't we used to debate that?"

"We probably did. We debated everything."

"You certainly made me work to keep up. The Rachel Korr short course in critical thinking."

There was a burst of static on the intercom and then one of the conductors announced that they were fifteen minutes from Philadelphia's North Station. Some of the passengers began to take their luggage down from the overhead racks. Ethan began to get up to pull Rachel's case down when she reached out and restrained him.

"There's still time," she said. "Is this going to be good-bye? Again?"

He nodded slightly and looked away, not sure what to say.

"Tell me something," she said. "Did you still care for me? When you saw me that last time, that Fourth of July?"

"You know I did. Desperately, the way you feel when you long for something and know you can't ever have it. I didn't dare show any of that. By then I knew you didn't see me that way, and I wasn't about to open myself up to your condescension or your pity."

"I would never have guessed that."

"It's the truth. Was the truth."

"Sometimes it's the words we don't say that do the damage. Funny how it works out." She took a deep breath, exhaling slowly before she spoke again. "So when did it wear off for good? When did you stop loving me?"

He shook his head, his hand on the handle of his briefcase, leaning forward, his voice so soft that she had to move closer to hear him.

"First love, Rachel," he said, "You were my first love. Does that ever end? At least not in our heads, it doesn't. How could it?"

"It's not that way for everyone."

"I can only speak for myself."

She didn't say anything in response, but slowly reached into the pocket of her suit jacket. She retrieved a business card from an elegant leather case, and silently offered it to him. Their fingers brushed when he took it from her.

"You know where I am, now. How to reach me."

"I do," he said.

"You still have what's left of the semester," she said. "If you want to get together again, that is, in New York. It's your call, Ethan, just like it has always been."

He didn't correct her version of their history—for it had never been that simple—but let the comment go unchallenged. "It sounds easy, doesn't it," he said. He ran his fingers gently along the raised type of her card. It was thick, an expensive card, heavy stock. "My mother used to quote something, 'God is good, but never dance in a small boat.' It'd be a small boat, seeing you again. I'm not sure whether I would want to take the risk of dancing in that boat."

"I didn't say it would be easy," she said. "I know it wouldn't be."

"It's your fault," he said, trying a lighter tone. "If you looked your age, then there wouldn't be any danger."

"Thank you. I'll take that as a compliment, true or not. And it's a lovely metaphor—dancing in a small boat."

"There's something else, too," he said. "That you should know."

"What?"

He closed his eyes for a moment, and when he opened them, he found Rachel there, watching him intently, waiting for whatever he had to say.

"Before, I didn't tell you all I should have. I didn't come clean. I have another child, a girl, Karen. Her mother was my girlfriend before Marisa. I didn't mention her earlier, because I'm not particularly proud about the situation. My daughter, Karen, is just about to start college."

"Are you close to her?"

"I'm afraid not. We're not in touch, not the way we should be. Karen's mother and I broke up when Karen was two years old. All my fault. Completely mine. I messed things up. It was when I was in graduate school."

"Hard feelings?"

"There were. There are. Marisa was the reason I left Sharon."

"I see."

"So it was messy. Sharon ended up with a really nice guy—they got married fairly quickly—and Karen considers him her father, not me. I wanted to tell you because I've got some baggage in the fidelity and fatherhood department. Badly done, as the British say."

"Did you think I would think less of you, Ethan?"

"You should. I do. The truth? The past ninety minutes with you makes me remember what being torn in two directions was like. I don't know whether I trust myself to keep the distance I should. Not that I'm assuming anything about how you might feel, Rachel."

"Don't you already know?"

He thought about Marisa for a moment, wondering whether she and Alexandro had finished dinner—she probably had made gallo pinto, a spicy dish of rice and black beans topped with salsa lizano, a meal that Ethan didn't care for, but that she and Alexandro liked. If they had finished, Alexandro would be in his room listening to music and studying (allegedly studying, Ethan would say to tease him) and Marisa would be watching television or, more likely, tackling the crossword puzzle. He pictured her sitting in their wingback armchair, a pool of light from the shaded antique standing lamp illuminating the folded newspaper, her reading glasses perched on her head, her brow furrowed in concentration. It was her daily test of her English, and she was proud when she completed the puzzle without having to ask Ethan for help.

He looked over at Rachel. They were so different, the two women he had deeply loved, both strange and exotic by the standards of his childhood. Who would ever imagined that Ethan Snowe, son of a New England police chief, would marry an artistic Costa Rican with dark brown eyes and a lilting, accented English? He wondered if he owed that leap of faith to Rachel, the notion that he should love whoever he pleased, whoever he damn well pleased to love? He suddenly felt, unexpectedly, a sense of sadness. When he saw a strange look on Rachel's face, and he knew it was because of his tears, tears sliding down his cheeks, abrupt tears that he made no effort to wipe away.

She reached out and touched his cheek softly, her fingertips brushing gently against his face, his tears. He closed his eyes, and then she took her hand away.

The train had begun to slow; it had entered the underground tunnel that signaled that they were nearing the Philadelphia train station. It meant they had only a few more minutes before arrival.

"Perhaps a rain check, then?" she asked.

"A rain check?"

"Why don't you consider my card your rain check?"

He nodded, the card still resting in his right hand.

"Did you know that I kept the key?" she asked. "All these years."

"The key?"

"The room key. From the hotel in Portsmouth. It's in my jewelry box, in the bottom drawer. I guess I notice it perhaps once a year—maybe twice a year. It always makes me smile. And shiver just a bit." She paused and looked at Ethan, measuring her words. "People do the damnedest things when they're in love," she said.

"That they do," he said, feeling the edges of her card on his fingertips. "That they do."

10

Whisper My Name

Stay, she implores. Don't leave just yet.

I wasn't about to, he says. I'd need to put some clothes on first anyway. I'm not about to walk out of here stark naked.

That's good. I want to be the only one who sees you stark naked. Stay a little while longer.

Are you feeling blue? Is that it?

Perhaps. Just whisper my name, she says.

We're all alone. There's no need to whisper.

But there is. Only I'll hear what you say. I want to hear it from your lips. Just for me.

You're being silly.

No, I'm not. It's not that much to ask, is it? Hold me close, and whisper to me, please.

Is that close enough? he asks.

Don't tease me, babe. Kiss me, and then whisper my name.

I guess I can do that.

And then I'll kiss you and whisper yours, she says fiercely. And we'll never forget this moment. Only I'll hear what you whisper, and only you will hear what I whisper. And we'll never forget it, will we?

When you put it that way, how could we? How ever could we?

Whisper my name.

About the Author

Jefferson Flanders has been a sportswriter, newspaper columnist, editor, and publishing executive. He is the author of *Café Carolina and Other Stories* and of the First Trumpet Cold War trilogy of *Herald Square*, *The North Building*, and *The Hill of Three Borders*.

www.ingramcontent.com/pod-product-compliance
Lightning Source LLC
Chambersburg PA
CBHW070533130626
46555CB00003B/1393